W9-BCM-600

When Robert, the new kid in school, invites Jerome to stay overnight one weekend, Jerome is delighted. A night away from home! Robert's apartment is so big, the boys can make all the noise they want. They can even watch TV late, because Robert's room is down a long hallway, far away from his parents' room.

But when it's time for bed, Robert takes out a pair of blue pajamas, and Jerome is uncomfortable. At his house he always sleeps in his underwear—a clean pair, of course! But how can he tell Robert that he's never owned a pair of pajamas in his life?

In this warm story about two young friends, Isaac Jackson creates a realistic picture of two different families and shows how their differences can be understood—and even enrich a friendship. David Soman's fine and sensitive illustrations bring the boys and their parents to life in a memorable tale.

SOMEBODY'S ≈NEW≈ PAJAMAS

by Isaac Jackson
pictures by David Soman

DIAL BOOKS FOR YOUNG READERS NEW YORK

This book is dedicated to the memory of my parents.
I. J.

To Greenie, my teacher.
D.S.

Published by Dial Books for Young Readers
A Division of Penguin Books USA Inc.
375 Hudson Street
New York, New York 10014

Text copyright © 1996 by Isaac Jackson
Pictures copyright © 1996 by David Soman
Designed by Julie Rauer
Printed in Hong Kong
First Edition
1 3 5 7 9 10 8 6 4 2

Library of Congress Cataloging in Publication Data
Jackson, Isaac.
Somebody's new pajamas/by Isaac Jackson;
pictures by David Soman. —1st ed.
p. cm.
Summary: When two boys from different backgrounds become friends
and sleep over at each other's homes, they exchange ideas
about sleepwear as well as about family life.
ISBN 0-8037-1570-6 (trade). —ISBN 0-8037-1549-8 (lib. bdg.)
[1. Pajamas—Fiction. 2. Sleep overs—Fiction. 3. Family life—Fiction.
4. Friendship—Fiction.] I. Soman, David, ill. II. Title.
PZ7.J13614So 1996 [Fic]—dc20 93-32213 CIP AC

The art for this book was prepared using watercolors.
It was then color-separated and reproduced
in red, yellow, blue, and black halftones.

JEROME HAD ALWAYS LIKED ROBERT, the new kid in school, even though he was tall, skinny, and usually didn't like to get his clothes dirty. If Robert made a joke, Jerome would be the first one to laugh and get everyone else laughing.

Jerome chose Robert for his side on the kickball team at recess. Robert was a good sport. Once, when he did fall down and tear a hole in the leg of a new pair of corduroys, he didn't make a fuss about it. He just jumped up, brushed the gravel from his knees, and he yelled twice as hard when it was Jerome's turn to kick.

One day Robert and Jerome were walking home from school together. "Would your parents let you stay over at my house this weekend?" Robert asked. "My mother said she'd take us out to dinner and a movie."

"Sure!" Jerome said. He figured his parents would probably say it was okay.

Jerome said good-bye to Robert outside of his apartment house and went upstairs.

"Jerome, don't run the hot water, okay, sweetie?" his mother called as he headed for the kitchen. The hot water must be out again, Jerome thought. He kissed his mother on the cheek and asked if he could help her do anything.

"Just keep the noise level down. The baby is sleeping. I swear I don't know what we're going to do about this building. We've been telling that landlord for weeks that the boiler doesn't work."

"Uh-huh," Jerome said as he walked out. He decided to wait until later to ask about visiting Robert.

The hot water had returned by dinnertime and Jerome helped his mother set the table. "I'm going to make you some banana bread for being such a good boy," his mother told him with a smile.

In less than an hour the bread was in the oven and a warm glow hung over the rest of the evening, over into dinner.

Jerome waited until the banana bread was nothing but two big smiles on his parents' faces. Then he asked about staying overnight at Robert's house.

Jerome's father got up and cleared the table. "Robert. Hmmm. Isn't he the boy you talked about having those fancy clothes? Well, I guess he's all right," he said.

By the time Saturday came, Jerome was very excited. A night away from home! Robert lived in a big brownstone. His family had the whole building to themselves. They weren't cramped into a five-room apartment like Jerome's. Robert had said they could play running games up and down the stairs and through the halls. The house was so big, they could even play indoors if it rained.

As Jerome was getting ready to go, however, his mother got all fussy and nervous. "Don't act as if you're too hungry at dinner," she told him. "Don't let them think we're not feeding you."

"Oh, c'mon, Mom," Jerome moaned.

"I know, child. Don't mind me. You go and have a good time with Robert. Tell Mrs. Williams that Robert is invited to spend the night over here too," she shouted down the hall as Jerome left. He smiled and waved good-bye, then stepped into the elevator.

Robert and Jerome went boating in the park, and sipped ice-cream sodas at a cafe under the bridge. They saw tall old ships go by and strained their necks trying to see the very tip-tops of the skyscrapers.

They had dinner with Robert's parents at a fancy restaurant and saw a scary movie.

At the Williamses' house Robert and Jerome were able to make a lot of monster sounds and watch TV late, because Robert's room was down a long hallway, far from his parents' room. At Jerome's house you could hear everything. Even on weekends Jerome's father sometimes had to get up early and go to work, so Jerome couldn't stay up late making noise.

Finally Robert's mom came to the door and said, "Okay, boys, lights out."

Robert and Jerome got ready for bed. After the boys washed up and brushed their teeth, Robert took out a pair of blue pajamas with white trimming. "Where are your pj's?" he asked Jerome. When Jerome didn't answer immediately, Robert added, "If you left them at home, I can lend you a pair of mine." Jerome didn't want to tell his friend that he'd never slept in pajamas before. He always slept in his underwear— a clean pair, of course.

Jerome cleared his throat before saying, "Umm, yeah, I guess I left my pj's home. If you wouldn't mind lending me a pair, that'd be great."

"Sure, otherwise, you'd have to sleep in your underwear!" Robert said.

Jerome felt uncomfortable for a moment. But then the silky coolness of the pajama top touched his cheek. The cloth felt great, and before going to sleep Jerome told himself that he would get his parents to buy him a pair of his own.

But when he asked about it after he went home, Jerome's father said, "A pair of what? Boy, you got to be crazy. Your mama and I are doing the best we can to keep you and your sister well-fed and clean. I don't have any money to waste on pajamas for you right now, Son."

Jerome went to bed pretending his underwear was really the smooth pair of red and black pajamas he'd worn at Robert's house. But for the next few days he was much quieter than usual.

On Sunday Jerome's dad was setting the table for a big family dinner. Grandma was coming to visit with two cousins from out of town.

The old tablecloth had a few holes in it and Jerome could still see the place where he had spilled a jar of cranberries last Thanksgiving.

"Why are you using that old tablecloth for Grandma?" Jerome asked.

"It may be faded, but I grew up with this old piece of cloth. There's been so much laughing around this tablecloth, it could tell its own jokes. This family has its own way of doing things. Grandma wouldn't have it any other way."

Jerome thought about it for a minute. He began to feel much better.

The weekend that Robert came over to visit was a good one. The boys had lots of fun. Jerome's father took them to the park to play

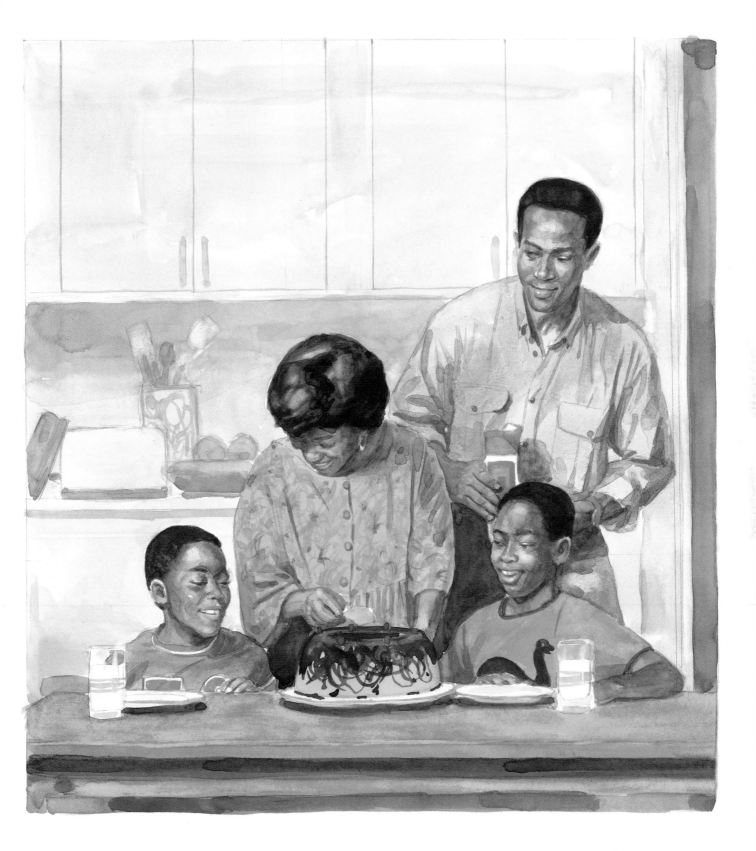

baseball. His mom made an extra-special dinner and baked a cake.

After eating, Mr. and Mrs. Bradley went into the kitchen to wash the dishes. Jerome took Robert into his room to unpack Robert's backpack.

"Oh, you don't need your pajamas here tonight," Jerome said.

"Thanks, but you don't have to offer me a pair of pajamas to sleep with just because I did it for you...."

"No, Robert, that's not what I meant. In my house we don't sleep in pajamas."

"What? Then how do you sleep?" asked Robert.

"In our underwear. Want me to give you an extra pair?" Jerome said it so matter-of-factly, Robert acted as if it was the most natural thing to do and left his pajamas packed.

A few months later, on his birthday, Jerome received a present in a big flat box. In it were two pairs of new pajamas. He changed into one pair immediately and paraded around the house.

"Somebody's new pajamas are a hit," said Mr. Bradley.

"They really are great," said Jerome. "But I think half the time I'm still going to sleep in my underwear, 'cause this family does things its *own* way."